Penis Vagina

This is a work of fiction. Names, characters, businesses, places, events, locales, and incidents are either the products of the author's imagination or used in a fictitious manner. Any resemblance to actual persons, living or dead, or actual events is purely coincidental.

<u>CHAPTER 1</u>

Several strands of it clung to her thighs between her legs.

THE END

CHAPTER 2

One might think this to be a rather graphic depiction from the ending of a pornographic book.

Not so.

But the date I'd brought to Granite Heart Bluff tonight thought it was pretty gross, and she wasn't thrilled. She called me sick, and wondered how I could end a presumable labor of love in such a way. Crystal never quite *got* my gimmicks and tricks.

"No," I told her. "You're missing the point. See, what I'm doing is some sneaky shit: Get a title with frequently searched words, shamelessly put the names of authors who are more popular in the search tool..."

"So you're just pissing people off. Won't that chase readers away from you?" she said, leaning back in the leather passenger seat as she smoked her cigarette. She knew I hated it when she smoked in my car, but she just didn't give a damn.

"I don't think so... I mean... I hope not. I did it thinking that fans and other authors might find it comical," I said, waving smoke away from my face.

"It's not comical," she said in a *too cool for you* fashion. So to remind her who was boss, I snatched the cigarette from her mouth and tossed it out the open window. It was so quiet up there that you could hear the fucking thing hit a rock, then quietly pat to the ground.

"Hey, fucker, what was *that* for," she said.

"You're hearing me, but you're not goddamn listening!"

She rolled her eyes before fixing them on mine. God, it made me want to hit her.

Continuing to stare into my eyes unblinkingly, she began rummaging through the rubbers and lubricants in her little purple purse, and broke her stare just long enough to light another cigarette.

"So," she began in a stoned tone, although she never had any drugs on her besides the Viagra, "what came first? The penis or vagina?"

She smiled playfully, the tip of her tongue pressing against the back of her upper front teeth, as she rubbed my semi- hard cock with a shoeless foot.

She was beginning to piss me off.

"Look, bitch, you don't know the first thing about the algorithm-"

"-Oh fuck. The algorithm. Here we go again," she rudely interrupted.

"Again, indeed. It's important to know how it works. There's more to life than simply knowing how to work a man's cock, you know."

"A *married* man's cock," she affirmed.

"You only suck married cock?"

"You're the only married cock for me, big daddy," she said, swinging her feet from my lap to the floorboard.

"Do you want to go home?" I said with a tight grip on the steering wheel. It was getting late anyway. The night always seemed to bring larger waves crashing onto the beach below the bluff. The later it got, the louder. And right about now, they sounded like bombs going off.

"Do you want me to go home?"

Was this a test? It sounded like a test, and, well, I never did like tests very much.

"What I want you to do is open your door and stick your head out," I said.

She scoffed.

"Fine. But no back- door this time. You're too big for that."

"No back door," I agreed, charmingly.

She opened the door and got on all- fours, so that everything above her tits were sticking out of the car. She arched her back to present. I glanced at her vagina, bald and razor-bumped. I wanted to gag.

"That's it. That's what daddy likes to see," I faked, and slowly turned in my seat so that my feet were in the air.

"Now do me a favor… and get the fuck out of my car!" I said, and booted her in the ass with both feet.

She launched from the car, and I immediately realized that I'd neglected to account for the downward- slope that I'd parked beside. She began rolling down it like a moron, and to my horror, straight for the cliff.

"Hey, you dumb twat! Stop rolling!" But it was too late. Her body disappeared over the edge. I could hear her screech for a few seconds, and then a jarring sound from her voice box as a dull *thud* echoed in the night.

"Goddammit," I said. I knew she wouldn't be missed. Most certainly not by the cops. But I did feel somewhat responsible.

I got out and walked to the edge of the cliff. Despite the moonlight reflecting on the water, it was too dark to see her.

"Crystal!" I shouted. "I'm sorry! Come on, bitch, let me know where you're at and I'll come get you and take you back to your hotel!"

There was no answer, and in my heart I knew she was dead. All I could really do was hope that the tide would come far enough in to claim her and pull her out to sea. I could see that happening.

"Fuck it," I mumbled, and went back to my car. To my knowledge, no one knew that we were together, so, oh well, I guessed. I like Crystal a lot, as far as whores went. But I'd find a new one. Shit, shopping around was half the fun.

*

As I crept into my home, I noted that Liv had left the doorway light on for me. She was sweet like that, always making sure I came home to a lit doorway, the thermostat set to just the right temperature, and dinner waiting for me in the microwave. I walked over to it and opened the door. Lasagna. Man, she made great lasagna. I punched in the cook time, the thing beeping at me in agreement, and started heating my food. Then I went over to the dining room table and opened my laptop.

I refreshed the stats page and perused the graphs and charts. To my glee, Penis Vagina had seventy- five new views and forty new purchases since this morning.

I should've raised the price, I thought, turning around to retrieve my dinner.

Once I set the table for myself, I noticed I also had a few new reviews. There were a lot of one- stars. I clicked one of them. The reader was upset because they felt click- baited by the title. To add insult to injury, the reader said the book had little- to- no plot development, and was rife with editorial errors.

"Yeah, well, I still got your money, fuckhead," I said quietly so as to not wake up Liv or the kids. Tommy was eight, and 'Nessa was six.

It was three o'clock A.M. and the last thing I expected was to feel Liv's hand cup my shoulder from behind. She must've been feeling frisky. It was typically the only reason she was up at this hour.

I closed my eyes.

"Not now, honey, I-"

I was spun around in my swivel chair and back- handed in the face, sending me to the floor. I got to my hands and knees and saw droplets of blood splash on the linoleum floor from my nose. Then every bit of air left my body as I was kicked in the stomach, sending me spinning over to re- position myself on my ass.

I began to protest, but a calloused hand covered my mouth and the ominous face of a man with crazy, spiraled hair leaned close with his finger to his lips, hushing me.

"You have a very beautiful family, Will. It would be a damned shame to wake them up with your wailing and hollering, and have to get them involved," he said.

Slowly, he removed his hand from my mouth, only lowering his finger from his lips when he stood up.

"What do you want?" I said, wiping blood from my nose with my sleeve. "I don't have any money."

"Wrong," he said in a hushed, gruff voice. "You have *my* money."

"What the fuck?" I was genuinely confused at first.

"Your wallet. Give it to me. Now."

I obliged, and he made me flinch as he swiped it from my hand.

"People don't like being click- baited, ass," he grunted.

"What?" I said, although I was putting two and two together.

"There was nothing to do with a penis *or* vagina besides one little insignificant mention of a vagina in that poorly- written piece of shit you passed off as a book."

"What the fuck are you talking about? Did you honestly think you were getting a book about sexual anatomy?" I was genuinely pissed, and it was a genuine question.

"Your other books feature it. Amputations and mutilations of dicks and pussies, not to mention the fucking. *Sex and violence.* Isn't that one of your taglines on the social media platforms? One of the hashtags you always use? I saw that and decided to give you a shot. I read one mediocre book, and thought this one might be better, but it's a total piece of garbage. I expected penises and vaginas." This lunatic was so upset that he was visibly shaking.

"So you decided to break into my home and rough me up?" I was in awe.

He smiled, one tooth missing in the front.

"That's the problem with you indies. You guys think you can just put out whatever the hell you like, marketing it as whatever the hell you like.

He began pulling bills from my wallet.

"Here's for the money I spent on your book," he began, pulling out a bill. "Here's for my gas. Here's for the wear and tear on my hand. And here's a surcharge for my troubles."

He tossed my wallet at me, hitting me in the chest. It still had bills in it. Business man. I liked him. Until he spit on me.

He turned away from me to leave, and what can I say? Pride and rage took possession of me.

There was a vase in the center of the dining room table. I ran to it, dumped the flowers out and sprinted towards the intruder. He must've heard me coming, 'cause he turned around just in time for me to slam the vase into his ugly face.

He shrieked like a woman giving birth and dropped down, hugging my knees. He definitely wrestled at some point in his life.

I fell down, smacking the back of my head. It dazed me, but not enough to keep me from jamming my thumbs into his eyes. He screamed out more in terror than pain, I think. He tried to back his head away from me, but I had a firm grip on it, as I felt my thumbs pop his eyes deeper into their sockets.

White and pink fluids ran down my hands, wrists and forearms.

"Oh my god!" came my wife's voice.

Liv. Shit.

"Honey, call the cops," I said, a lot more calmly than I would've expected.

As I heard her oblige, my assailant grabbed a handful of my balls and squeezed with everything he had. I turned and flipped him off me, immediately mounting him. As I began raining down punches, I saw his eyelids open a couple of times, exposing what was left of his mangled eyes, set impossibly deep in their sockets.

I was shocked when his hand slipped into the back of my pants! His fingers wiggled around in there, and when I felt my asscheeks part, I knew exactly what he was trying to do. This motherfucker was trying to stick his hand in my asshole.

He managed to get the tip of one finger in before I grabbed handfuls of his spiraled hair and began repeatedly slamming his head into the floor. Each dull thud sent pangs of nausea through me. But my rage overcame it.

"Will! You're killing him!" I heard Liv scream.

I looked at her talking on the phone, then over to the hallway where Tommy and 'Nessa were crouched against the wall, holding each other, tears in their eyes.

I looked down at the asshole. He turned his head to spit out a tooth, and I could see a massive opening in his scalp, pink, fleshy chunks stuck in his matted hair.

He began snoring loudly, his body heaving and convulsing with each breath.

Was I going to jail? I wasn't. They'd never take me alive. I could just… go to the bedroom… get my handgun from the top shelf of my closet… solve the problem right here and now.

Jesus.

Was that a real option? Of course it was. I could take my life anytime I liked. But here and now seemed like it would be a bit hasty. Better to at least see what my options were.

I could already hear the sirens, and looked at the intruder to make sure he was still breathing. He was, but as I stood up and backed away, I watched the broken fuck's brain matter leak out the back of his head.

My wife, our children, my household... we'd be violated, and a new rage was welling up in me. My family as witnesses or not, my sanity slipped for a moment, and as I heard the first police car approaching, I ran to my little friend, swung my leg back, and kicked him with everything I had, planting my foot into the back of the top of his skull. When I say *into*, I mean it entered his head, all the way to my ankle.

A mangled eye shot from its socket, leaving liquid oozing from whence it came.

As I tried to remove my foot, it wouldn't come out and his head simply slid across the floor. With his afro- like hair, it was like trying to mop up a bloody floor with no fresh water.

The first police officer had arrived at my door, kicking it in, and aiming his gun at me.

"Disengage!" he screamed.

I tried to shake Mr. Shitbag off my foot, but he stayed stuck to me and shook with my foot, shaking his body all around like he was having a seizure.

"Disengage, motherfucker!" the cop demanded.

I turned around and pointed my finger at him like a dagger.

"Look, asswipe, I'm trying-"

A deafening blast erupted as the cop discharged his weapon. I flew backward, spinning, my foot coming out of the shoe that was still lodged in fuck- face's head.

I fell to the ground, feeling as though I'd been punched in the shoulder. Then three, possibly more, cops were upon me. I felt my neck pop under the weight of a knee. My lower back spasmed from the weight of another knee, and I was hit from head to legs with fists and sticks amid screams to put my hands behind my back.

My arms were pinned underneath me, unable to move with so much swine on top of me.

Finally, one of my arms was yanked free from beneath me and placed behind my back, where my wrist was squeezed so tightly with handcuffs that my hand instantly tingled and then became numb,

Same with the other arm.

The clicking of boots walking across my floor made my stinging eyes open. My reflection greeted me in shiny, polished leather. I felt like I was in a concentration camp; all beat up by men with sticks and uniforms with shiny boots.

"Mr. William Adair, I presume?" a voice said, eerily calmly. I looked up from the shoes to see a warm smile underneath a short, trimmed mustache. "You don't look as scary as I thought you would."

"Not trying to be a scary person," I said, and deliberately sprayed blood from my nose, speckling his pristine boots.

He brazenly knelt down beside me. He was holding a cup of coffee. I could smell the authority from it. He inspected my shoulder, and we both knew it was only a flesh wound.

"Well, hell, son… you've generated some reports," he said.

"W- What do you mean?" I said through gritted teeth, the knees still crushing my neck and back. I felt a stick rudely jab me in the ribs. "Owe, you fucking piglet! One- on- one, you and me, shit for brains!"

This resulted in more sticks all over my body, with shouts for me to *stop resisting* echoing throughout my home.

"Daddy!" I heard 'Nessa cry out. I looked over at her, and she continued screaming from the shock of seeing her father beginning to look like a Dawn of the Dead reject.

"Alight, boys, I think our famous author here knows his place," Mr. Mustache said.

As Nazis began to climb off of me, I said, "I don't think *Author* suits me. Maybe just *Writer*."

Mr. Mustache looked at his soldiers from left to right, before looking at me and bursting with laughter. The infusion of coffee and cigarettes on his breath was disgusting.

"Ok, writer. Here's the deal. We're taking you on a little ride," he said.

"Ah, fuck. Will it be a long ride? 'Cause I get carsick," I said.

He continued to smile, and grunted out a chuckle. Then he slapped me in my head with his wide- open palm. My head snapped to the side. He was treating me like a misbehaving step-child. I suppose he would've purposely jostled my hair, if I had any. I also suppose he would've used it to pick me up off the floor. Instead, he bunched up the back of my shirt so that it choked me, and got me to my feet.

Still choking me with one hand, he used the other to point at the fuck- stick's corpse. Chunks of brain matter were still slowly leaking out of his head around my shoe.

"Now… I don't know what's going on here, but that is one dead fuck. That boy's deader'n' sheeit. And we're gonna get down to the bottom of this-"

"-That motherfucker was only here because-" I began, but was cut off by Mr. Mustache clamping a hand over my mouth, stifling me.

"Shh… not here," he bizarrely whispered into my ear, nearly pressing his lips to it. "Let's go down to the station.

CHAPTER 3

The halls were cold, and my torn shirt did little to protect me from its icy bite.

Mr. Mustache was gone. He'd turned me over to a short fat security guard who was now imploring me to enter a brightly lit white room, where only a circular table and three chairs awaited me.

Fat- stuff brought me in and sat me down.

"Alright, buddy, now listen here… I'm gonna take these cuffs off. Try pulling any slick shit, and your ass will be tazed. Got me there, good buddy?" he said. Despite threatening me, there was a pleasantness to his voice and overall demeanor.

"Aye- aye, captain," I said, feigning utter joy like a complete jerkoff.

I must say, when the first cuff came off and I was told to put it on top of my head, I had half a mind to turn around and grab for his non- existent neck to see if there was a windpipe somewhere in there.

But I did as I was told. Then, a crazy thing happened. As my other hand was freed and placed on top of my head, Fat Stuff began screaming at me and backing away with his hand on his tazer. I suppose if this police reject was an actual cop, his hand would've been on his gun.

"Don't fucking look at me! Face away from me, or I'll fill you with volts! Stand down! Stand down!" he shrieked, his fat face becoming red.

I did as I was told, in shock, until I heard the door open and close behind me.

Just as calm as he'd been before his awkward screaming episode, he said, "Ok, you can turn around now. Detective's Humphreys and Bristol will be in here to talk with you shortly. Go ahead and have a seat."

I liked Fat Stuff better when he was being nice.

I'd no sooner begun to sit down when a man and woman walked in, and I caught myself mid- squat.

"No, no, go ahead and sit," said the man with a wave of his hand. "We're gonna be here for a while. I'm Detective Bristol, and this here is my partner, Detective Humphreys."

He was thumbing through a file as he spoke, while Humphreys slapped hers on the table and stared into my eyes with an intensity that said she either wanted to fight me or sit on my dick.

"Oh jeez. Oh, man," Bristol said. "I'm sorry to be the one to tell you this, but the man you got in a scuffle with... he's passed."

"Well, no shit, Sher-" I began.

"You will only speak when spoken to!" Humphreys shouted.

"He *was* speaking to me, Tits," I said, the name referring to her large, middle- aged breasts.

"Do you want me to bring C.O. Dillon back in? 'Cause I'll bring him back in!" she shouted.

"Oh, you mean Fat Stuff? I like Fat Stuff. He's a good kid," I said, un- phased.

Just as Tits was about to pipe up again, Bristol cut her off.

"Let's just start from the very beginning. What happened," he said, nervously tapping his pen on the table.

"Ok, so I wrote this book called Penis Vagina..." I began.

"Hold up," Tits said, and looked at Bristol. "Did he just fucking say he wrote a book called *The Penis Vagina*?"

"No *the*. Just *Penis Vagina*," I corrected.

"She looked at me out of the corner of her wide, bloodshot eyes, although she was still facing Bristol, her hands bladed. "That's what I said."

"No, you said *The* Penis Vagina. It's just two words: Penis Vagina," I insisted.

"Who cares what penises or vaginas-" Bristol began, his pen tapping quicker on the table.

"Alright, you know what? Fuck penises and vaginas," Tits said, shaking her head and grabbing her file.

"Yes, that's what they're generally for," I said.

She looked like she was going to hit me, and very well may have, if it weren't for Bristol moving things along.

"Ok. So you wrote a book called Penis Vagina," he said calmly.

"Yes. I published it through Phantazmazon. It was an experiment, really. I wanted to see if my views would go up because of the name, and even if I added the tagline '*A Mean-Spirited Horror Novella*' if my sales would out- perform my previous efforts.

"Sick fuck," Tits said, slowly shaking her head, being melodramatic again.

"Sound reasoning," said Bristol, and Tits scoffed at him. "So... how'd we get here to this point, with you being accused of caving in a man's skull and killing him?"

"Well, the things in the book had nothing to do with penises or vaginas. And to many, that's considered click- bait. Then, we take it one step further, and people purchase it and find a total lack of penises and vaginas and they feel, say... ripped off," I said.

"So then what was the story about," said Bristol, ceasing his pen- tapping only long enough to ask the question.

"It was just some weird fucked up shit I threw together. Drivel, really. The reviewers are gonna have a field day. *'This guy shouldn't write.' 'This is why it's so hard to find a good book these days.' 'Now everyone thinks they're a writer.' 'Do we not edit anymore?'* You know... things like that. They think they're editors just as much as I think I'm a writer, so... whatever."

"Ok," said Tits. "Let's get to the-"

"The dead guy. Yeah," I interrupted. The bright overhead light was starting to make me hot, and I could feel beads of sweat forming on my brow. Was I getting nervous? Really, I'd felt pretty numb after the cop car ride. In any event, I continued.

"Well, all I can really make of that is that the lunatic was angry he was click baited, wanted his money back, and tried to take it. But a sale's a sale, and I wasn't about to give up jack shit."

"So this death could've been avoided for how much, exactly?" said Tits.

"A buck ninety- nine."

Tits scooted her chair around the table and leaned close to me with her hands between her knees.

"You know what I think?" she began. Her mouth sounded sticky, and it grossed me out. Then a waft of some pretty gnarly coffee- breath hit me. I dry- heaved once. I can't stand shit like that.

"You alright?" Bristol said.

Without letting me respond, Tits continued.

"I think you're a liar, a cheat, and an asshole."

I sat upright, and then back a little, with a shit- eatin' grin on my face.

"What kind of an insult is that? Are we in the wild west, Tits?" I said.

"We're gonna nail you to a cross," Tits said through clenched teeth. I was glad that she at least kept her mouth shut this time.

The door opened, and Fat Stuff's head peaked in as a dread came over me. They really meant to twist this like Cheese- Dick's death was somehow unjustified.

"Anyone want coffee?" Fat Stuff asked.

"I noticed that Bristol had stopped tapping his pen as he looked over at him.

"No, we're good. Thanks," Tits said, also looking over at him.

But I wasn't looking at him. I was fixated on Bristol's pen, held limply between his fingers.

I could go to jail for a long time. Could I go for life?

As my anxieties grew within me, my knee began to bounce uncontrollably, but too subtle for Tits or Bristol to notice. I kept looking at Bristol's pen. The ding- a- ling was about to drop it.

"Alright, just let me know if you guys need anything," sweet Fat Stuff said.

Then, it happened. Like slow- motion, it happened. The pen dropped. I was so fixated on it that I can tell you it flipped once. Then it tapped the floor like growing thunder in my ears.

And I made a decision.

"Here, let me get that for you," I quickly blurted out, and before any of them could protest, I got out of my seat and kneeled down to grasp it. Then it was in my hand like a knife.

I grabbed the edge of the table and flipped it over on its side. There was a commotion, and I didn't know what Bristol or Fat Stuff were doing, but I knew exactly what Tits was doing. She was pulling her gun from its holster.

Everything continued to play out in slow motion until I put my plan into full engagement.

Now everything seemed sped- up.

I punched Tits in one of her tits. I guess it's because I remember punching my sister in one of her tits in our teens and her recoiling in such pain. It didn't work as well on Tits' tit, but it worked well enough. Her weapon was unholstered, but she stumbled backward and it discharged into the ground.

Then I was upon her, one arm wrapping around her neck, the opposite hand pressing a pen firmly against her carotid artery.

Everyone stopped in their tracks. Bristol was to the side of the doorway. Fat Stuff was directly *in* the doorway. Bristol held up one finger, while his other hand pointed his stubby gun at me.

"Wait, wait, wait..." he said. "We can fix this. I promise you that we can start over. I know you're under a lot of stress..."

"Jesus. That load of horse shit is bigger and stinkier than the fucking book all this is over," I said. "Just keep real calm, or this pen rapes the inside of her throat."

"Alright, alright!" Now Bristol's hand was held out in a *stopping* gesture. Fat Stuff's eyes were shifting between the two of us.

As I slowly made for the door, I said, "Move to the side, Fat Stuff." He did as he was told, moving as slowly as I, his hand on his tazer.

I simply nodded at Bristol. He began to switch places with me, and the closer we got, the more vivid my next plan of action became. After all, I was royally fucked now. After I got myself out of this little jam- out of this precinct- I decided that I would steal a bottle of whisky, go home to retrieve my pistol, say goodbye to the family, and take my happy ass to Granite Heart Bluff to spray my brains into the ocean mist. I would do it standing right at the edge, so that my body would fall to the beach beneath. None of this *miraculous-second-chance-at-life* bullshit. I never much liked life anyway.

Bristol and I were in position now during our little dance where we were facing each other, me inching closer to the doorway, him slowly moving away from it.

When we were directly facing each other, I made my move.

Driving the pen into Tits' artery was a lot easier than I'd anticipated. Motherfucker should've brought a ball- point for me to struggle with.

As Bristol ran towards me, I ripped the pen from Tits' neck and cocked her head to the side, spraying blood directly in to

Bristol's eyes. As I dropped her to the floor, I also dropped at the sound of Fat Stuff's tazer discharging.

The tazer's prongs glided just above my head, missing me by inches.

Bristol was on the ground holding Tits. Not literally tits, but Tits the woman. Blinded with blood, he sobbed her name.

"Humphreys. Come on, girl, stay with me," he cried like a bitch. "Help!"

The shout seemed to put Fat Stuff back into motion, running directly toward the massive, growing puddle of blood between the two of us. I backed into the hallway, and started running.

Just as I began my sprint, there was a sound that reminded me of the meatheads at my gym when they dropped the barbell to the floor after a heavy set of rows. It caused the whole hall to shake. I briskly jogged backward to look into the interrogation room one last time, and found Fat Stuff on the floor, face- down, a growing pool underneath his head reaching to intermingle with Tits' blood.

It was a damn shame. I liked Fat Stuff.

I ran to the corner of one of the adjacent hallways and crouched down as I heard the first set of footsteps running my way. As they were about to round the corner, I stuck my leg out. As the cop tripped over my leg, I realized he'd already unholstered his weapon. It flew out of his hand as he hit the floor, his chin bouncing off of it. I was pretty sure I heard his teeth clack together, possibly breaking them.

Not much to tell here, as I wasn't fucking around or taking chances.

I picked up the cops .45 caliber handgun and placed it against the back of his head as he tried to get up. When I pulled the trigger, some of the blood and pieces of brain sprayed back at me from the hole in the back of his head, but most of what got on me was what flew from the gaping maw that his face had become, splattering on the floor beneath him and back at me.

This shit was getting way out of hand.

From around the same corner of the cold, white, bleach-smelling hallway, came a petite female cop. She was skin and bones, and I knew I could overpower her. Plus, in these milliseconds of frantic ponderings, I realized that for whatever reason, the bitch still hadn't drawn her gun.

Luckily for me, she literally ran right into me. I quickly wrapped an arm around her neck and put my gun to her head.

"Listen," I said to her, almost a whisper in her ear, "Just don't do anything stupid and you might... *might*... make it out of this alive."

"You're fucking up your whole entire life. Let me go, and I'll consider dropping the *Kidnapping* and *Assault With A Deadly Weapon* charges," she said.

I chuckled.

"The two that were questioning me… I've killed one of them," I said with a smile.

"There are plea bargains," she said, desperately.

Many more cops began to peer into the hallway from around the corner, and speaking to me all at once so that I had no idea what the fuck they were saying. I counted eight. What the fuck were they all doing here? Shouldn't they be out patrolling? Rescuing a kitten or beating a minority or something?

"Look at all this tax- payer money hard at work," I said.

"Let her go!" a steroid- ridden officer shouted.

"Simmer down, there, Roids. I'll let her go once I'm out the door."

"What do you want?" said another lanky cop.

"To leave. Duh. Dipshit," I said, and scoffed.

I came fully into the adjacent hallway and waved the gun to indicate that I wanted them to step aside.

I pulled the stick- figure officer tightly against me, and pressed the gun hard against her temple.

"You're hurting me!" she said.

"Good." A simple reply, but it got my point across.

We moved down the hallway, and I could hear the shouting of several men. We were in a male cell block.

As we neared the iron- barred door, the yelling became louder, until I could finally see the maniacs. They were at the door like rabid dogs, climbing over one another. Was this a jail, or a fucking nut- house?

I continued my back- stepping down the hall, insulted by no less than fifteen men, as the police officers kept a steady pace with me, guns drawn. When my back hit a wall, I looked to the side, were there was what looked like a circuit breaker. It was labeled into three sections: *'closed'*, which the lever was currently set on. Then *'manual'*, and finally *'open'*.

The piggies were right next to the holding cell door. I looked over at the group of inmates.

"The first one of you motherfuckers that steps out of this cage will be shot in the balls. Try me, motherfuckers," I boomed.

Everyone, piggies and inmates alike, stared at me blankly. I tried to maintain looking cool. Tough.

I whispered into the stick- figures ear, "What the fuck's everyone's problem?"

I was delighted that her response was also a whisper.

"They don't understand what you're doing. They don't know why you're just standing here looking stupid."

"Oh."

Then I remembered we weren't friends.

"Switch it to *open*, you stupid bitch," I said.

She did as she was told, and a tatted- up musclehead immediately ran out and towards me, where the exit was.

The redirection of my line of fire was swift, and way more accurate than I would've thought. I grinded my teeth as I pulled the trigger. I imagined the popping sound was the inmates nuts busting open, and it made me laugh, shrill and phlegmy. I'm sure that I sounded psychotic. Good. Maybe I was.

The inmate grabbed his crotch, and toppled over, screaming.

"There are more of you than little ol' me. Shit, between you shitbags and the piggies, there are probably between twenty- five to thirty of you, but I swear to fucking Christ I won't go down quietly. Now... who's the next martyr?" I spoke the truth. I wasn't playing.

Nobody moved, as their eyes pierced my flesh to see that my soul was not fibbing.

"Who are the betas, and who are the piranhas?" I asked with a smile.

"Shit," said the guerilla cop.

"That's right," I said, and waved my piece from the piggies to the cage a couple of times.

"Ain't happening, slick," said an older, hardened looking cop. "Now why don't you-"

I capped him in the top of his scalp, the bullet spreading his balding head apart.

"Captain!" a younger rookie- looking asswipe screamed out, and made a move towards the screaming Captain, who was attempting to push together his spread scalp. His efforts were in vain, as his fingers repeatedly slipped across his flesh from all the blood so that he couldn't get a good grip.

As the rookie neared him, I let off another round at the good old Captain, and wouldn't you know it? The bullet found its way right in between the separation that the previous one had made.

Then I popped a round at the rookie. It tore through the cartilage of his ear, and grazed the back of his head. It was a poor shot, but it got my point across.

He shrieked in pain, cupped his ear and slid his ass back several feet, using his legs, smearing blood beneath him.

"Jesus fucking christ, you guys." This was getting old. "I don't know how else I can show you that I'm not fucking around. Get in that fucking cage!"

More hesitation.

I indiscriminately put a round into the center of the face of a cop who'd been standing quietly up until this point. He let out a brief scream, clutching at the hole where his nose used to be, before crumbling lifelessly to the floor.

The next round was so lucky that it was a direct hit into the eye of another.

I surveyed the remaining cops, all ghost- white and sweating as they all were, and tilted my gun in the direction of the cage.

"In," I said.

With many sighs, grunts and grumbles of my would- be captors, they finally filed into the cell. When they were all in, I told Sticks to close it. She did as she was told.

Roids glared at me as he grasped the bars.

"You're not gonna get away with this shit," he said, and he no sooner ended his sentence when a tattooed homie of an inmate pulled his gun from behind him.

Roids turned around in a flash to try to snatch it back, but Tats simply tossed it to a bearded lumberjack- looking inmate. The other cops raised their guns at him.

When Roids, screaming with rage, went after the lumberjack, the gun was tossed to a messy- haired greaseball of a guy, who blew off Roids' right hand, sending fingers between the bars of the cell.

Gunfire erupted from the gang of cops as the inmates moved in on them.

"Time to split, Sticks," I told my petite piggy.

<u>CHAPTER 4</u>

The morning sun stung my eyes, and the air was cool enough to see my breath as the autumn temperature fought against summer.

Sticks and I had descended one of two sets of stairs, and were standing on a smooth concrete slab, my arm around her neck, my gun against her head.

Below the second set of stairs, a woman pushed a stroller along the sidewalk, while another walked in the opposite direction, reading a book that was probably not Penis Vagina.

Beyond the sidewalk was well- maintained grass amid several trees, where a teenage boy and girl sat on a bench holding hands and giggling.

It made me want to vomit.

"Hey!" I shouted, and popped a round into the bench between them. They jumped, with mortified expressions on their faces. "Get to school!"

The couple ran, and I was amused that they went in opposite directions. The lady with the book simply dropped it and fled, and the woman with the stroller left behind a high- heeled shoe as she hurriedly pushed her stroller, wailing.

"I think we're alone now, Sticks," I said into my captives ear almost seductively. "Lose the belt."

With a slight hesitation, she unsnapped her belt- keepers and let them fall to the ground. Then she let her duty belt do the same.

Her earpiece became unplugged from her radio, the cord stretching from her ear, so that the screams from the holding cell could be heard over it. Gunfire could be heard erupting, as well as pleas to put the gun down.

But the most damndest thing of all was the laughter.

I caught a momentary glimpse of my captors glossed lower lip quivering.

"Oh, no tears, Sticks. This will be over soon. On your knees," I said, with a wave of my gun. She did as she was told.

I stepped close to her, my gun aimed at her head.

"Well, Sticks, it's been real. But it looks like this is where you get off. The ride's over," I said.

She looked directly into my eyes- my soul- with a wild stare.

"Don't look at me," I said as I raised the gun to her face. Her eyes seemed to bulge, glistening with un- spilled tears.

"I said don't fucking look at me!" I commanded, but insubordination was all that was returned.

I almost felt remorse.

Almost.

"I ain't got time for this shit, I said, the sun glaring off the silver slide of the gun as I looked down its sights. In her final moment, I thought her eyes might pop out of their sockets, but they stayed put as blood sprayed from the back of her head and left a speckled v- shaped pattern behind her, the tip of the V pointing towards the back of her head and spreading out of there in a million speckles like a blood- filled water balloon had hit the ground just behind her.

Her body tried to balance for a few moments, rocking back and forth, wide eyes fixed on mine, before slumping over onto the ground. Blood gushed from her nose like two wild rivers. Between the rivers and the hole in the back of her head, she lay in an ever- growing blood- pond, quietly rippling at the concrete shore.

"Aye, man!" came a young man's voice from behind me. I turned to see a rusty- haired guy in his early twenties, wearing jeans and a t- shirt, holding a copy of Penis Vagina.

"Yes?" I said, acknowledging the absurdity of the intrusion with sticks spilling out all over the place in front of me.

"This book, man..." as he neared me, I felt the insane urge to pop some of his pimples. "It falls... you know... kind of short, man."

"How do you mean?" I said, my head twisted around with my body still facing Sticks, gun in my hand as her pond grew and grew.

"I mean, I've read all your books. I love all the nudity, sex and violence. This book has violence, for sure, but for a book called Penis Vagina, you'd think there'd be some hardcore fucking, cum- slinging, maybe some genital mutilation, those kinds of things. You know… like your other books," he said with absurd confidence, given the fact that I'd just killed a cop in front of him.

I relaxed my pistol and held it limply at my side.

"Look, kid, there's more to lo life than just *hardcore fucking* and *genital mutilation*…"

"But the thing is…" he cut me off "We fans have come to expect that from you."

I chuckled.

"Fans? You mean all three of you?" I said with a smirk. But the smirk fell as I saw men, mostly in their forties, and mostly fat with stringy hair begin to emerge from behind the building, behind trees, and the like. There were also females, many who appeared in their twenties, dark rings around their eyes… it looked like a zombie apocalypse movie. One of them walked up the stairs with a copy of my book.

Before I knew it, I was surrounded on all sides by men and women of various ages, making themselves known.

"We hear you were taken in," said Pimples, thumbing the precinct. "We came to get some of our own questions answered. Is this what we are to expect from you now?"

"No, I…" I looked all around me. No way this many people came to see me. I must've been hallucinating. I didn't remember the last time I'd slept. "… This was a one- off."

"That's what you did last time. I fucking *one- off*. Maybe let us know next time, so we don't have to fill our garbage bins with this kind of garbage," Pimpled said.

I was tired, drained and confused. My head was spinning.

"No, that would... defeat the point..." I managed.

"What was the point?" one stringy- haired greaseball said. He began walking towards me, along with Pimples, and the others followed suit.

"I think the point was to fuck us," Pimples said.

"Trying to fuck us?" the Greaseball said.

I ran my hand across my sweaty, stubbly head. This couldn't be real.

"There wasn't even much of a plot," a voice said from behind me. I turned to find an attractive girl dressed in all black standing there, and as I backed away from her, I bumped into another man, large, bearded and wearing overalls.

I looked up and stared at the sun with my mouth open. The colors melded together: yellow, orange, blue, purple. Then I buried my face in my fists, one of them still gripping the gun.

After rubbing the sun from my eyes amid murmurs and accusation, I came to a determination.

"You're not real," I said, and pointed the gun with one hand, the other still covering my eyes. The gun discharged and the warm blood that splashed on me felt real enough. My assumption was wrong.

I swung around and capped Overalls in the gut, before shooting the girl in black in the jaw. Her head snapped to the side. After a moment, she slowly looked at me and tried to speak, her jaw hanging lower than where it should, her tongue hanging freely between a large gap where her teeth used to be.

I fired again. The round hit the other side of her jaw, ripping it completely free. She fell to her knees, holding her face, oceans of blood rushing between her fingers.

I was spun around by the shoulder to face a Greaseball.

"This is the way that you treat your fans?" he screamed into my face, and took a swipe at it with a forward- curved paring knife.

"Fuck you!" I screamed, and blasted the wrist of his knife-hand, severing it and sending it to the ground.

He screamed as he grabbed his stump and stared at me with bewilderment.

I chose one of his eyes and shot it, point blank. I could see what I can best describe as spaghetti exit the back of his head, before he smacked onto the ground. I picked up his knife and placed it into my belt.

"Oh my God, he's shooting us!" one of the crowd members shouted.

"Get him! Get the gun from him!" screamed another.

"Where are the fucking cops!" a third shouted.

"They're busy," I said, running down the remaining steps.

I'd never been much of a runner, so perhaps it was pure adrenaline that allowed me to outrun the mob that was now pursuing me down the street.

I fired several shots into the crowd, and laughed out loud when I saw several people trip over the fallen bodies. Circus music played in my head, and I just kept running.

<u>CHAPTER 5</u>

The motel room was dirtier on the inside that out, and smelled like cat piss and cigarettes despite being billed as a non-smoking room. There was cheesy wallpaper on the walls that had seen better days, with a hole here, a tear there, and all stained a sickly yellowish color.

I set my six- pack on the dresser, took off my jacket and threw it on the bed, along with my gun, and went over to the bathroom sink.

As I washed blood from my face, I wondered if the mob had my address. I'd purposely run in the opposite direction of my home, and when I'd carjacked that poor fucker at the streetlight, I'd continued in the same direction. If someone did have my address, I could only hope they'd leave my family alone when they didn't find me there. Plus, maybe there were still cops there, it being a homicide scene and all.

I finished sloppily rinsing my face, rubbing my fingers through my stubble. As I pulled my cheeks taught, downward, I looked at my eyes. They were a hazy red, with pronounced vessels.

When I returned to the main room, I continued to examine myself in contemplation as I cracked open a beer, but as I began to chug, something in the mirror caught my eye. A man in a black suit walked past my window. In the light of the noon- time sun, the man, whose hair was immaculately styled, was wearing sunglasses and I couldn't tell if he glanced into my room or not.

In any event, I dropped my beer to the floor, letting it spill all over the shitty carpet, sprinted toward the window and threw the drapes closed.

I could hear the clicking of the man's dress- shoes, and my asshole puckered when they stopped just outside my door.

Slowly, I reached for my gun on the bed and picked it up. What the fuck was such a well- dressed man doing at such a seedy hotel such as this? Whatever the answer, I felt minor relief as I heard his shoes clicking away.

And just like that, I was back at the dresser, and opened two cans of my cheap beer. I chugged one until it was gone, without taking a breath. When I was done, I felt the urge to belch, but only foam came up. Three- quarters of the way through the second one, the foam came back up again with a vengeance, and I leaned over the small waste bucket by the dresser.

A large, steady stream of foamy vomit cam up, followed by a massive belch. Then more, acidic, vomit came up, and when it was gone, I began to dry- heave. I thought I heard the sound of the man's clicking shoes walking passed my door again, but the dry- heaving was relentless, and the slightest bit of shit forced its way out of my asshole under the pressure.

I clenched my ass- cheeks tightly, so as to not soil my underwear, and after a few more heaves, I stiffly walked to the toilet and sat down. I held one hand on my sweaty head, and the other limply held the pistol between my knees as relief came.

I realized that I had not eaten today. There was nothing to absorb the alcohol, and I remembered seeing a hotel diner when I booked my room. I decided a greasy burger was just what the doctor ordered.

I wiped myself and briefly inspected the mess that I'd made in the toilet before flushing and washing my hands. I tucked the gun down the front of my pants, concealed it with my shirt, and left the room.

As I tried to look nonchalant walking across the roadway among the parking spaces, I saw the man in the suit out of the corner of my eye, about five rooms down from mine. He was sitting in one of the green plastic chairs which were outside every room, wearing his sunglasses with one leg across the other and an open newspaper in front of him.

I wanted to look at him a little harder, but I couldn't. My eyes were naked, and I didn't want him to catch me staring. I needed a hat and pair of sunglasses. Maybe there was a gift shop.

From what I could tell, he wasn't looking at me, but those fucking sunglasses... who knew?

I approached the diner and when I opened the door, the sound of sizzling and the smell of meat made my stomach rumble. There were a few people in there, mostly elderly, and I was relieved that none of them seemed to pay me any mind.

I also noticed a gift shop on the far side of the diner with sunglasses and baseball caps in plain view.

I sat on a stool at the counter and waited for almost twenty minutes for my order to be taken after being poured coffee that I didn't ask for.

CHAPTER 6

My belly was full, but not too full for beer, I thought as I made my way across the parking lot. I caught my reflection in the rear windows of parked cars. I was wearing my new red- and-white hat with the slogan *'Eat Pussy'* across the front of it, along with my new gold- rimmed aviators, pushed close to my face beneath the bill.

I'd also bought myself a can of chew, a large pinch of which I placed in my lower lip. As I sucked at the tobacco and spit out the saliva like a pro, I noticed that Slick wasn't sitting in his chair anymore.

I stopped walking and looked around. No sign of him anywhere.

"Well ain't this some fuckery," I said under my breath, and spat again before venturing closer to my room.

I stopped at my door, almost standing flush against it, looked both ways, and inserted the key into the keyhole.

That's all it took.

Without even turning the key, the door slowly creaked open, and the key slid out. I held my breath, my heart thumping in my throat as I tried to choke it back down.

I inhaled slowly as I watched my shoe slowly push the door. After a few inches, the door slowly creaked open on its own. I spit some chew- spit into the doorway, I guess in an attempt to solicit some sort of reaction. It padded softly onto the dirty carpet.

I scanned what I could see of the dimly- lit room. There. In the reflection of the glass of a cheesy framed painting of some tulips, there sat a human figure on the chair at the small round table to the right of the doorway, in the corner.

I looked both ways down the sidewalk to make sure no people were present, lifted my shirt, and pulled the bulky pistol out from the front of my pants. Then I took a hard, sharp breath in through my nose and let it out through my mouth. I ran into the room, immediately turning to my right and raising the gun.

There sat the man in the suit, still wearing his sunglasses, with one leg crossed over the other. He calmly looked up at me over the top of the newspaper he'd been reading.

Aiming my gun at him from across the room and sweating profusely, I spit what was left of my wad of chew onto the floor, and bluntly asked, "Who the fuck are you, Slick?"

Very delicately, he folded up the newspaper and placed it on the table. Then he clasped his hands together as he regarded me with the slightest tilt of his head.

"My name is Larry. Larry McDaniels. I represent Phantazmazon, and you, my friend, have been causing quite a bit of grief for us, I'm afraid," he said with a gruff voice.

"Oh yeah? And how's that?" I said.

He took off his glasses and set them on the table. Crows-feet- a- plenty, to say the least. He leaned forward in his chair, squinting at me, his eyes coals buried in wrinkles and a thousand years of scowling.

"Penis Vagina?" he said, the words dripping with disdain.

"Yeah. Pretty clever, huh?" I said in a cocky tone.

"Ok. For a second, let's ignore the obvious inappropriateness of the title."

"Hey, wait just a cocksucking minute. You guys are the ones selling dildos and hardcore erotica, chief," I said.

He shook his clasped his clasped hands at me a couple of times during his next argument:

"Yes, but the name... it's misleading."

"What's in a name?" I said. "Never judge a book by its cover, right?"

He adjusted himself to sit upright and straightened his suit jacket.

"The bottom line is that thousands of people search for things along those lines, and then they get this."

"Sounds like their problem, not mine," I said. The gun was becoming heavy.

His wrinkles bunched together to make a wincing face.

"But even your key search words. You have dirty words-"

"Penis and vagina! I cut him off again. Those are standard words of the male and female anatomy!"

"Fine. But you have other authors names in there."

"Yeah, everyone does that. And these authors write some pretty horrific shit. So do I, typically."

"And you haven't here?"

"There's no sex. No sexual gross- outs. No genital mutilation. What the fuck's the big goddamn deal?" I was getting sick of this asinine conversation. My trigger finger was getting itchy.

"Alright. I'll cut right to the chase, then. Penis Vagina," his yellow teeth were clearly visible as he apprehensively said the title "has been removed from our site.

I felt myself losing it. My gun trembled. My face hurt from my scowl. It was just a book. But it wasn't just the book. It was the principle. It was hypocrisy. It was the hurt and frustration and pure anger that my book… my *art*… was being taken down for reasons that were complete bullshit, while the site proudly sold Blue Wigglers with the G- Spot Rabbit and Anal Extenders.

All this got the best of me. After all, I'd been killing all day anyway.

My first shot tore his face apart right down the middle, causing one of his black coals to pop out of its socket, proving that it was, indeed, an eye.

But I kept popping caps.

My grouping was a little off; an ear torn off here, a scalp coming free there, and before long, there was simply no trace of where any face used to be. Now there was simply a pouring, chunky mess, as my condescending little shit sat leaning forward in his chair.

After a few more rounds to the top of Slick's head, the slide of my pistol locked. It was spent.

Fuck.

I really should've thought to conserve ammo. I should've thought to grab some spares from the piggies back at the precinct. I should've controlled my temper.

I turned my head, tossing the gun to the ground, put my hands on my knees and heaved up what I'd just eaten onto the floor. Fuck it. It wasn't *my* floor. Shit, I didn't even try to make it to the waste basket.

When I was done, I stood more or less upright, wiping my mouth. I regarded Slick. He sat there looking at his lap, a robot of a human, blood pouring nonstop from the collective hole in his face, framed by shredded chunks of skin. An ear was missing. The other one was hanging on by crimsons threads.

The pressure rushing to my face from the violence of my vomiting caused my mucus membranes to protest in the form of dual crimson fountains flowing from my nostrils.

I wiped it with my forearm, leaving a large red paint- stroke across it. Then I went to the bathroom.

I reached across the toilet for the paper and pulled out a sizeable group of sheets, wading them up and putting them to my face.

As I stopped the period coming from my face, I looked in the mirror and happened to notice that this cheap ass hotel hadn't even bothered to put a curtain on the shower. Figured. You get what you pay for.

When I was satisfied that my blood- flow had finally stopped, I turned on the faucet, and stooped over to splash water on my face, scrubbing off blood.

Exhausted, weak and gun- less, how much longer was this going to go on? I found myself yearning for my family, and although there was no one else around, I was glad my tears were concealed by the water.

I took in a deep breath, turned off the faucet, rubbed my eyes vigorously and tried to compose myself.

Slowly looking at my reflection, I noticed how red and puffy my eyes were. Just as I caught a final tear spill, I caught the reflection of a guerilla- man holding a plastic shower curtain behind me. He was dressed exactly like Slick, right down to the cheesy fucking glasses.

As I mused over the fact that I'd solved the case of the missing shower curtain, it was placed over my face, and the Guerilla pulled it taught. When I tried to gasp, the plastic from the curtain entered my mouth instead of air.

The panic made it worse. So did the physical exertion. I flailed about, but Guerilla was strong and relentless, pulling the curtain tight around my face.

I reached back and grabbed a handful of Guerilla- nuts. As I squeezed, he made a noise that was something between a growl and a scream right into my ear, and pulled the shower curtain so tight around my face that I could feel my smashed nose begin to bleed again.

Balls of steel, I supposed.

I scrambled in my pocket, trying to find the keys to my stolen car so that I might puncture a hole in the shower curtain and be able to breathe again, but I found something better: the paring knife from the crazed fan from earlier.

I removed it from my pocket and pushed the lever so that the spring- assisted blade flicked open, reached up and punctured a hole in the curtain at my mouth.

After a few gasps, my senses came flooding back to me. I dropped to my knees and tucked my chin into my chest. The result was Guerilla sliding up over my shoulder and landing head- first onto the hard tiled floor.

He lost his grip on the shower curtain, and I stood up, the hook- like blade of the knife pointed upward and at the ready. Almost as quickly, he stood up with blood trickling down his forehead.

I brought the blade back, the swiped it forward and upward, slicing clothes and flesh with ease, from the bottom of his stomach to mid chest.

He looked down, dumbfounded, and ripped his shirt open, buttons popping and falling on the floor. He held his bloody hand in front of him as if beholding a miracle. His skin was open wide, but a membrane, streaked with droplets of blood, was holding his organs in place.

But the miracle began to fade.

The membrane began to bulge, and organs began sliding over one another. The Guerilla tried desperately to push them back into place. When that failed, he grabbed the edges of his torn- open torso and tried to pull the wound back together. But this only squeezed the organs against the membrane, and before long, it tore open.

As his insides began sliding and dropping out of his body, he looked at me and ripped the sunglasses off his face. His eyes were half- open as he looked into mine, and he began to sway back and forth. Finally, he collapsed to the ground, the rest of his guts spilling out into a heap of pasta.

I straightened my hat, which had somehow not fallen off, grabbed my sunglasses and put them back on. Then I spit on my mess of a friend.

CHAPTER 7

The car was parked right outside, and with no belongings besides my four remaining beers, I immediately jumped in and began driving with no destination.

Cracking open beer number four, I checked the speedometer and made sure not to go more than five miles over the speed limit as began chugging.

I drove for several hours, up and down familiar streets, past homeless camps, and observing drug deals here and there. The beer gave me a warm feeling of calm that was deceptive. I knew it was a false sense of comfort, yet I welcomed it, nonetheless.

The first drops of rain began hitting the windshield at four o'clock PM, when I pulled into the gas station. The attendant was annoyingly ecstatic to fill up my tank. I tipped him early. Ten dollars, to be exact. With six beers in me, I was feeling more generous than usual. I needed a refill for both my gas tank and my liver.

I entered the gas station convenience store and headed straight for the cooler, where I grabbed a case of beer. Fuck it. Why not? The reality that my life was over was setting in. I was a killer. Killers always seemed to get caught. Especially the ones whose identities were known.

I had no plans on going to Mexico, and when I'd been driving for all those hours, I'd come to the conclusion that my death would only be on my terms. But I needed to see Liv, Tommy and 'Nessa first. Say goodbye to them. Tell them I love them.

I set the beer on the counter and told the clerk what pump I was on. He ran my credit card. It was declined. I took my aviators off and set them on the counter, pinching the bridge of my nose and squeezing my eyes shut.

"Look, man, there should be a couple grand on there," I grumbled.

The clerk ran the card again, and shook his head.

"I'm sorry, sir. It's not working," he said reluctantly.

I looked into his eyes, my blood pressure rising, the thought that it wasn't his fault being the furthest thing from my mind.

I reached my hand back and saw the clerk's pupils dilate. The young man never stood a chance.

I swung with everything I had, missing his chin and connecting with his throat. He grabbed it and fell backwards into product racks, sending packs of cigarettes, vape cartridges, cans of chew and other assorted items flying all over the place.

When he landed on his ass, he curled up in a fetal position, choking, gasping and whimpering.

"Will that cover the charge?" I said.

He muttered something I couldn't understand, so I figured he agreed. I grabbed my case of beer and exited the store. Once outside, I ripped open the top of the beer box and grabbed one of the bottles so that the bulkiest part was protruding out the top of my fist.

"Got a receipt for me?" the attendant gleefully asked.

"You've been working hard. Here. Have a beer," I said as I brought back my hand and flung the beer at him. It smacked him right between the eyes with a *clinking* sound, ricocheting off him and shattering when it collided with one of the pumps. The young man went down, unconscious.

I wasted no time getting into my car that wasn't really mine and taking off, the tires raising a stink as they skidded off the asphalt. I looked in the rearview mirror and cursed myself for having left my brand new pair of sunglasses on the counter, as several people came to the attendant's aide.

<u>CHAPTER 8</u>

There was plenty of crime tape around the perimeter of my yard, but not a cop in sight. I figured they were restoring order at the cop shop.

The tape was covered in rain that had since ceased to fall, and the droplets looked like millions of tiny stars on a canvas of reflective black, white and yellow.

And how about that? Someone left the fucking door open. At first, I thought that maybe there was a chance that my family could still be in there. But I wasn't about to rush in to sunshine and rainbows squeezing the last twenty- four hours from my eyes like they were all a bad dream. After all, I was surely plastered all over the news at this point. Did I have myself thinking that the feds or whoever the hell took up cases such as this were just going to let my wife and kids walk freely? Of course not. They'd frozen my assets, took my family from me, and made sure I wouldn't be able to take a piss without having to look over my shoulder.

So much for goodbyes.

The hinges on the car door protested as I opened it, got out, and slammed it shut. I pulled my hat snuggly in place, and waited for any type of reaction, more angry than sad at this point.

You could hear a church mouse drop a crumb of cheese in the silence, and I listened to my hand rub my stubbly face as I approached what I used to call home.

The first thing I noticed was that the motion- sensor light didn't come on, and sure as shit, when I reached inside the doorway, the switches did nothing either. Someone must've flipped the breaker. I'd found my way in the dark plenty of times before.

I went to the spare bedroom, not running into a single thing. I opened the closet doors and could faintly see the tube I was after: a long, waterproof canister designed to be a part of a bug- out assortment. This one had a revolver and twelve gauge short- barreled shotgun with a pistol grip in it.

I unscrewed the tube and out came the guns, and a large knife, fishing gear, first aid kits and other survival supplies onto the guest bed. I threw the shotgun strap around my shoulder and double- checked that the revolver was filled to maximum capacity.

Truthfully, the shotgun was for me, and the revolver was for anyone standing in my way. Sure, there were a few rounds total in the shotty, but I began looking at it more and more like a sacred object. My means of self- deliverance. My beacon to remind me that even if the time and place should not be right amid the growing chaos, it was still my faithful companion. My sentinel.

I heard a metallic *clinking* sound from the opposite corner of the room, followed by a brief, intense glow and the sound of tobacco burning furiously before the lighter was once again capped.

There, sitting in the plush chair, smoke escaping his mouth, was the Paver. He was called the Paver because for us indie hardcore horror writers, he'd paved the way. If there'd been one stand- out person among all the others, specifically *extreme* horror writers, who tested waters, pushed envelopes and showed the rest of us that if you wanna play you gotta pay, it was him.

"Taking the easy way out, or blasting one?" the Paver asked.

I tucked the revolver into the front of my jeans. The Paver wouldn't soil his hands with me. Too much class.

"Maybe a bit of both," I said.

The Paver stroked his scraggly facial hair with a slender, tattooed hand. "Death does find a way of increasing the value of the deceased's work."

"Penis Vagina? Shit, Liv and the kids will be lucky to get a couple day's lunch money out of that thing," I said.

"Why'd you write it, Will?" the Paver said calmly.

It was the question of the day, yet still managed to take me by surprise.

"I guess I just wanted to see what would happen," I said, placing another dip in my lip.

"Simple as that?"

"Simple as that."

"And was it worth it?" the Paver said, lowering his head at me.

I sucked hard at the wintergreen flavored wad of tobacco in my mouth and spat saliva on the floor. Fuck it.

"Fuck it," I said.

"You know why your peers are pissed?" the Paver asked, cocking an eyebrow and taking another drag off his cigarette.

I bunched my shoulder.

"No. I really don't."

"I'm speaking of the indie writers… they put time and effort into their craft…" he said.

"But not the editing skills," I interrupted. "Lord knows I don't. "

"They market the hell out of their books, which come purely out of the darkest recesses of their minds. They come up with blurbs and catch- phrases, create hype and clout, and whether someone thinks you're a good writer or a shitty writer… you've totally disrupted this rhythm. They feel as though you cheated."

"Hey, man," I protested, "No one wrote these rules."

"You don't have to convince me of anything," the Paver said. "But people like Porky here, are a little upset."

He thumbed the direction behind me.

I spun around, the ice- axe that had been bought for an excursion which never happened barely missing me, and was immediately pulled from the mattress.

Of course, a guy like Porky was upset. With titles such as 'Non- Consensual Ejaculation' and 'Rub One Out On Your Thigh In My Hometown', he was probably upset that *he* hadn't come up with 'Penis Vagina' himself, especially with its search engine perks.

He swung the axe horizontally, and I had to suck in my gut to not get a nip/tuck. The axe cleaved the drywall deeply, and seemed to be stuck.

I took advantage.

While Porky's mass hulked over the axe handle, trying to free it, I pulled the revolver, took aim at the crook of his arm and fired. The effects were devastating and fantastic. He let go of the tool and squeezed his arm, now being held by threads of fabric, and who knew how much meat. Maybe none. He let out a shrill cry.

He must've loosened up the ice- axe just enough for me, because when I grabbed its handle, it came free with minimal effort.

I swung it with all my might as Porky hunched over screaming about his arm. The tapered blade penetrated the back of his neck and burst out his mouth, sending teeth in all directions, riding strings of blood.

Though he jumped at being speckled with blood, the Paver nonetheless put his cigarette in his grinning mouth and clapped excitedly.

I yanked on the tool a few times, trying to free it before realizing that I didn't need it anyway.

I grabbed the shotty and nodded at the Paver. I wasn't going to kill him. He was the GOAT. Besides, he hadn't tried to kill me.

I got what I came here for.

That was good enough.

But evidently, that wasn't good enough for Pat East, for when I entered my living room, she stood in the doorway, blocking my means of a hasty exit. It seemed all of the more popular indie authors wanted my ass tonight. And this bitch wasn't fucking around.

With her long hair moving ever so slightly in the breeze, and her simple black t- shirt and matching pants, I must say she looked pretty badass as she leveled her AR at me.

As you can imagine, I couldn't admire this bit of badassery for very long. I had to get the fuck out of the way, and did so just in time to hear the ear- piercing crack of the gun, instantly followed by the sound of the bullet whizzing past me and striking the wall behind me. It sent a cloud of dust falling onto the couch beneath it.

I found myself behind the recliner.

"Give up?" I shouted, and was answered by a round going through the chair, dangerously close to my ass. "Jesus! Why are you so pissed?"

"You wanna sit there and use my name as a key word for your shitty little clickbait book? Yeah, that doesn't sit right with me," Pat said, and fired another round through the chair that concealed me. This one skimmed the top of my *Eat Pussy* hat.

"So you try to kill me over it? What the fuck is wrong with you?" I said.

I was on my knees, and the next round that went through the chair struck the floor so close to my balls that I thought I got a man- scape. I knew it was only a matter of time before one of the bullets would strike me.

Then I got to thinking. She had the big badass gun. But it would only shoot a specific, precise target. Me? I had buckshot with a nice spread. I wasn't gonna let her get off another round.

I pumped my shotgun, stood up, and shot in her direction. As I hunkered back down, I heard her agonizing scream.

I peaked over the back of the recliner. She'd dropped the AR and was bleeding from her mid section. She went to grab the gun again when she saw me, but I was quick. I pumped the shotty again and fired at her, blowing the top of her head clean off, sending skull fragments and bits of brain everywhere. When she hit the ground, more chunks clumped out of where her scalp used to be, and I gagged at the scene. Not only was her brain spilling out, but the buckshot had done a number on her face. Not wanting to stand there and admire my handiwork any further, I fled the house.

<u>CHAPTER 9</u>

As I sprinted across my un- mowed front lawn, I only vaguely acknowledged the nearing headlights.

"You motherfucker!" a voice screamed from the Bentley. Of course. Why not? It seemed to be the wish of every- fucking- one these days.

I was like a retarded deer in the headlights. I couldn't make up my mind which way to jump, until it was too late. The car didn't hit its breaks until well after it hit me, sending me several yards away, and the shotgun out of my hands. *Why didn't I just shoot the driver?* That was the first thought I had as I slid across the road.

I was vividly aware that my ribs had cracked, and of my shirt shredding along with the flesh beneath it.

I slid for what seemed like forever, until I ended up next to a grey, rusted piece of shit El Camino.

The Bentley had stopped, and now two other cars joined it on either side. I rolled to my knees and spit up some blood. Evidently I had some internal injuries. Maybe my fucked up ribs were stabbing something.

As I clumsily got to my feet, I heard car doors opening. I looked up to see two figures get out of one car, and one out of each of the other two. At first, their faces were hard to make out, it being night and all, but as they neared me, my jaw dropped.

Traditionally published authors. Best- sellers at that. Steve Harker flanked the left, with his white button- up shirt and suspenders over his slightly muscular shoulders. He held a cigar between his teeth.

The middle left was Robert Prince, silver- haired and with beady eyes that pierced me behind rectangular spectacles.

Then there was Clint Bootz with his shaggy brown hair. And smiling! The prick was always smiling!

And last but not least, there was Sloppy Joe. Sloppy Joe was Robert Prince's son. People called him Sloppy Joe because that's what he was compared to his father.

We'll leave it at that.

Harker wasted no time pulling his gun and firing in my direction. The sound made me fall back on my ass and I found myself sitting up with my legs apart, and I felt everything in my crotch shrivel into almost nothing as the bullet hit the asphalt just inches from it. What was with people trying to shoot me in the nuts?

"No! It can't be as simple as that!" Prince shouted. "We need to make an example out of him."

I wasn't quite sure what *that* meant, but it sounded jacked up enough to jog my memory of the forty- four Magnum in my pants. I quickly calculated my rounds. It was a five- shot. I always kept one cylinder empty as a safety precaution, and I destroyed Porky's fat- ass arm with one. Three rounds left, and four motherfuckers. If I shot three, maybe I could get close enough amidst the chaos to tango with the fourth.

I clutched the gun and withdrew it from my pants, scraping the root of my dick as I did so. I winced and grabbed myself, causing me to hesitate.

Harker took advantage of my hesitation, and blew away my kneecap. I grabbed my knee with my free hand and rolled to my side, screaming. I'd never felt so much pain in my life, up until that moment.

In my vulnerable state, I heard one pair of footsteps from the lynch mob hasten.

I lifted my spinning head and saw Bootz rushing toward me with eager hands. I swung my gun- hand up, aimed for his face, and pulled the trigger.

At first, I was unsure if I'd hit him. His body swung away from me, the coattails of his black trench coat following him. His hands were at the side of his head.

Yes, I had shot him. But he wasn't down.

"Son of a bitch!" he cried out, and before I knew it, Harker and Sloppy Joe were upon me, Harker grabbing my left arm, Sloppy Joe trying to control my right by the wrist.

I began flailing and kicking, but something about getting hit by a car takes a lot of the fight out of you.

Under all the pressure and stress, I couldn't help but to clench my hands into fists. The problem was that my finger was still on the trigger. The gun discharged another round. My eyes squeezed shut from my stupidity. Another wasted bullet. Shit. One round left.

But I ain't no bitch, and would not go quietly.

As Harker and Sloppy Joe hunched over my flailing body, my gun- hand came loose, and I spun around on my back and jammed the barrel of my pistol between Harker's sack and anus. His head snapped back in pain. I pulled the trigger and the bullet must've gone straight through his body and out his mouth, 'cause his face turned into a fountain of blood, raining down on Sloppy Joe.

"Aw, fuck!" said Sloppy Joe, as he backed away.

After a couple moments, Harker's body stiffly tipped over like a felled tree. When his body hit the ground, his head slapping the road, blood pumped from his mouth a couple more times, and then a steady river flowed from it.

"Grab him!" Prince said.

Bootz let go of the side of his face to look at him. His ear was missing.

"What?" he said.

"Grab the fucker!" Prince insisted.

"What?" Bootz repeated.

"Oh, for fucks sake," said Sloppy Joe, and he lunged for me.

I aimed my gun at him.

"Stay back, you bargain- bin motherfucker!" I screamed.

He stopped.

"Don't listen to him! He's bluffing! He's out of ammo!" Prince shrieked.

"What?" Bootz said.

"How can I know for sure?" said Sloppy Joe.

"Fuck around and find out," I said, relentless with my lie. It was my only option.

Bootz, not hearing anything that was going on, marched straight towards me like something straight out of an eighties monster movie. Now I was terrified and irrational, and pulled the trigger several times.

Click.

Click.

Click.

Bootz back- handed the gun from my grasp, and I heard the metal bounce off the ground in the distance. Not a second later, he was grabbing me by the collar of my shirt and dragging me towards his car.

I punched and kicked with my good leg, my limbs finding nothing but air, my shirt ripping to shreds, until Bootz let go of me behind his car to open the trunk.

I started moving away from it, army crawling on my elbows and pushing myself with my good leg, until I felt someone grab the ankle of the leg with the blown- off kneecap.

"Just where do you think you're going, dumplin'?" I heard Sloppy Joe say.

He yanked on my leg, snapping it backwards as I slid towards him, my open wound grinding against the road. When I was back to the car, Sloppy Joe lifted me by my wrists and Bootz clamped a firm grasp on my balls.

Through all the screaming and wailing, I don't think I cried up until this point. But I was sure as shit crying now. I was sobbing like a baby as I was lifted up by my wrists and nuts and swung into the open trunk.

Bootz grabbed the hood, and leaned over me. His speech was a little fucked up, I assumed because he couldn't hear himself, but I could understand him loud and clear.

"Think you're smart, huh? The Click- Bait King. Every king needs a crown. I got something for you. It's perfect, trust me. I made it just for you," he said through clenched teeth.

Somehow I suspected it wasn't macaroni art as he went around the side of the car and opened the door. It wasn't but a few moments before he was hovering above me again with quite the item: a barbed wire halo.

Now, a barbed wire halo might seem a bit expected and cliché', but this had an extra little surprise. Between each barb was a double- edged razor blade, the wire going through the holes in the middle where you affix it to the handle.

I violently shook my head as Sloppy Joe lifted it, and I could head Prince chuckling in the background.

I shook my head even more violently as Bootz slid the crown over my brow, but stopped with the blades and barbs began to imbed themselves in my flesh. The further into my skin they penetrated, the higher the octave my screams became.

Bootz pulled a zip tie from his coat pocket and threw it around my wrists and through the trunks latch, securing my hands to it. With a violent pull, he secured it so tightly that a tingly shock-wave shot through my hands, all the way to my fingertips.

It was at this point I knew I was fucked.

"Alright. Let's get the fuck out of here. We're off to Granite Heart Bluff," Sloppy Joe said to Bootz.

"What?" Bootz shouted.

Sloppy Joe shook his head at him and slammed the trunk.

Despite the excruciating pain, the adrenaline dump and darkness, along with pure fatigue had me out like a light almost instantly.

CHAPTER 10

I've always loved the ocean. Especially the sounds of the waves crashing against rocks, the water lapping at the shore and being sucked back out to sea. The seagulls. The foghorn off in the distance. It's all mesmerizing and beautiful happy horseshit until the trunk opens, and Bootz yanks you out onto the ground.

I was wheezing.

I don't know how long I'd been out, but a quick survey across the land and up the rocks told me that we were on the beach below Granit Heart Bluff. Prince and Sloppy Joe stood side-by- side smiling at me. Sloppy Joe nodded to his right, and when I followed the direction I saw some sort of wooden contraption just beyond the front of the car.

"For the Click- Bait King," Prince said with a brief raise of his eyebrows.

"Let's take a closer look," said Sloppy Joe, and he grabbed the ankle of my bad leg and yanked. It was the damndest thing. You'd think I'd pass out from the pain of my remaining pieces of tendons and ligaments being torn apart, but looking up at Sloppy Joe holding my leg, then down at the blood pumping mess of where it had been my whole life... it was surreal.

That's when I think I first began to have my out- of- body experience, because man, let me tell you, I saw my own face turn ghost white as Prince wrestled his belt off and handed it to Bootz, who used it as a tourniquet.

I guess they thought I was still *there* enough that they didn't want me to bleed out before completing what they had in mind for me.

In a way I was.

In a way I still am.

I was looking down at the situation from above, just as I am now.

There was some sort of argument between the three of them, before Sloppy Joe finally sat me up, reached under my arms and clasped his hands together in front of my chest. I must've stunk, because he turned his head to mimic dry- heaving.

He dragged me to the front of the car and that's when I saw from my above- perspective what the wooden contraption was. There, next to a hole in the ground the size of the bottom beam of the contraption was a large crucifix, which they laid me on.

Feverishly, Sloppy Joe and Bootz worked on either side of me, wrapping heavy rope around my wrists. Then Sloppy Joe opened my hand, and his daddy knelt beside me with a giant nail and placed its tip in the palm of my hand. He brought up a mallet and let it drop down onto the nail's head.

In my all but blissful consciousness, a bright light flashed, and there was momentary pain, before I regained my perspective from up above. He brought the mallet down again, with the same results, and when he did it a third time, I felt my head snap back and the back of my aching head hit the crucifix, imbedding the razors and barbs deeper into the back of it. I, of course, screamed.

My earthly reality all came rushing back to me at once. My brow ached and stung sharply at the slightest shift of my facial features. My broken ribs and organs ached. Intense pain arose and simmered with each throb of where my leg used to be, and I couldn't move my fingers on my hand that was nailed to the cross.

As Prince made his way to the other side of me, I desperately tried to pull my hand free from the nail, but it was no use. The rope around my wrist prevented it. I couldn't even do anything with my other hand, futile as it might have been regardless, because of the rope.

Again, Prince knelt down, placing the tip of the nail into the palm of my hand. He brought the mallet up. I snorted and collected snot and blood in my mouth. The hammer dropped, sending what felt like a wave of electricity through my body.

I screamed and squeezed my eyes shut. When I opened them, the mallet was already up again. I spit the wad I'd collected at Prince's face. It hit his glasses, and drooled off of them.

At first, it was as if he didn't even notice. He simply hesitated bringing the mallet down. Then he turned ever so slightly towards me and without looking me in the eyes, let the mallet fall again.

It landed directly on my mouth, and I began choking and gagging on teeth, trying to bring them up to spit them out. I finally decided it was a lost cause, and I swallowed them. I was going to die anyway.

The mallet came down on my hand again.

And again.

I looked at Bootz as I screamed. He was still fucking smiling.

"Alright. Get him up there," Prince said.

As the two bozos began sliding my crucifix toward the hole in the sand, I saw Prince searching the ground until he found a sharp stick.

When we got to the hole, they struggled to shimmy the bottom beam into the hole, while hoisting me up, and when things aligned enough, the bottom of the cross slid into the hole on its own. When it hit bottom, it jarred me, sending my entire body in such agony that when I tried to scream, I vomited and shit myself.

"All hail the Click- Bait King," said Prince, as he walked towards me. He thrust the stick forward and it entered my side. When he yanked it out, a geyser of crimson followed.

I felt my head spinning out of control and whether I passed out or died right then and there, I guess I'll never know, 'cause I regained my overhead perspective.

Sloppy Joe was walking to the crucifixion from the open trunk, holding a gas can. Furiously, he started splashing my body with it. Then he stood back in line with the others, and Prince lit a match. He looked at it for a long while, before tossing it on the crucifix.

It instantly went up in flames, and the trio began clapping as though they were applauding someone's acceptance speech for some writing award. Dainty claps and snake- like smiles.

I watched for a good, long while, until my charred torso came free from my arms and leg, and Bootz walked over and pissed on it. But when I looked away, something else caught my eye.

There, amid jagged rocks, was a familiar face. Red, glittered hair. A too- short purple skirt revealing a bald pussy. Matching little purple purse.

Crystal.

Her head was almost completely turned around, but it was her. Her bones were clearly broken in many places, some poking through her skin, and her limbs were awkwardly positioned like a drunken yoga instructor.

She was covered in coagulated blood.

Several strands of it clung to her thighs between her legs.

The End

Instagram: William_T_Adair
Email: William.T.Adair@Gmail.com
Twitter: WilliamTAdair@WilliamTAdair

www.ingramcontent.com/pod-product-compliance
Lightning Source LLC
Chambersburg PA
CBHW061623130726
47996CB00003B/1103